For Lola
Q. G.

For Susan, my fairy princess
D. J. P.

We Both Read: Thumbelina

Reading Level (Child's Sections) – Gr. 1

English Translation/Adaptation Copyright © 2007 by Treasure Bay, Inc.
Illustrations © 2007 Quentin Gréban
French Edition © 2007 Mijade Publications (B-5000 Namur - Belgium)
All rights reserved.

We Both Read® is a trademark of Treasure Bay, Inc.

Published by Treasure Bay, Inc., 40 Sir Francis Drake Boulevard,
San Anselmo, CA 94960 USA

Printed in Belgium

Library of Congress Catalog Card Number: 2007920849
ISBN-10: 1-60115-007-5, ISBN-13: 978-1-60115-007-3

We Both Read® Books Patent No. 5,957,693

Visit us online at: www.webothread.com

Parent's Introduction

If you are reading this book with a child, you can read it aloud like any other book. However, this *We Both Read* book is also formatted so you can invite a beginning reader to read the book with you. If you are sharing the reading, you can read the sections marked with a ∞ "talking parent" symbol and then invite your child to read the sections marked with a ∞ "talking child" symbol.

As you read, you will notice that some words, which might be more difficult for your child, are first introduced in the parent's sections. You can recognize these words by their **bold lettering**. You may find it helpful to point these words out as you read them. You may also find it helpful to read the entire book aloud yourself the first time, then invite your child to participate in the second reading.

With books at five different reading levels, there are *We Both Read* books perfect for pre-readers, as well as for beginning and reluctant readers! Sharing these books together will engage you and your child in an interactive adventure in reading! It is a fun and easy way to encourage and help your child to read—and a wonderful way to start them off on a lifetime of reading enjoyment!

Thumbelina

By Hans Christian Andersen

Illustrated by Quentin Gréban

English Translation by Elizabeth Bell

Adapted by Sindy McKay

Once upon a time there lived a lonely couple who longed to have a child. A kind old woman **gave** them a seed and, with a twinkle in her eye, told them, "Plant this seed in a flower pot and see what happens."

The couple planted the seed and waited to see what would happen. What happened was astounding! At once there grew a large, lovely flower. The wife thought the flower was beautiful.

So, she **gave** it a kiss.

The flower burst open and inside sat a pretty little girl, no bigger than a thumb. For that reason, they named her Thumbelina.

Thumbelina's parents took good care of her. They made her a cradle from a nutshell and used rose petals for her covers. They were very **happy** to have Thumbelina.

She was very **happy** too.

One night, as Thumbelina lay sleeping peacefully in her nutshell bed, a slimy old frog **hopped** in through the window. The frog saw pretty little Thumbelina and declared, "Croak! Croak! What a fine wife this small girl would make for my son!"

The frog grabbed up Thumbelina in his slimy webbed hand . . .

. . . and **hopped** away.

The frog took Thumbelina to meet his son who lived on the muddy banks of a stream. "This will be your husband," the father frog told Thumbelina. "You two will live here in the mud together once you are married."

"Croak! Croak!" was all the son knew how to say.

How dreadful for Thumbelina! She did not want to live in the mud and she most certainly did not want to marry a frog!

The father frog placed Thumbelina on a lily pad in the middle of the stream and told her the wedding would take place the next day.

She was not happy now.

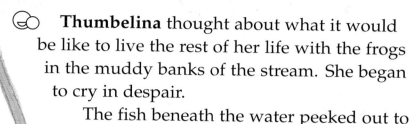

Thumbelina thought about what it would be like to live the rest of her life with the frogs in the muddy banks of the stream. She began to cry in despair.

The fish beneath the water peeked out to have a look at the sad little girl above. They felt sorry for Thumbelina and decided to try to help her. Taking turns, they began to nibble at the stem of the lily pad. It took most of the night, but at last the lily pad was freed. It began to quickly float down the stream, carrying Thumbelina away from the frogs.

Thumbelina was free.

Thumbelina continued to float down the stream. **Birds,** perched on the branches above her, seemed to **smile** down at her as she passed. "What a dear little girl!" they sang.

The **birds** made Thumbelina **smile**.

A gorgeous butterfly landed on the lily pad and asked if she could help Thumbelina. Thumbelina attached her sash to the butterfly and the butterfly eagerly pulled her even farther away from the frogs. Thumbelina felt safe at last.

Just then, a June bug flew by and saw the pretty little girl. He dove down, snatched her up, and began to fly back to his home. Thumbelina was terrified! But she was even more concerned for the butterfly still attached to the lily pad. She begged the June bug to take her back so she could free the butterfly, but the bug was mean and would not listen.

The bug took Thumbelina to his home and gave her milkweed to eat. She did not like the milkweed. He told her he thought she was the most beautiful thing he had ever seen.

She did not like the bug.

The other June bugs did not think Thumbelina was so beautiful. They laughed at her and said she looked like a human being!

The June bug, who had carried Thumbelina off, was beginning to think that the other bugs were right. Thumbelina wasn't so beautiful after all. He did not wish to keep her any longer. He snatched her up again and **flew** down to the bottom of the tree where he put her on a daisy.

Then, he **flew** away.

All summer long, Thumbelina lived alone in the forest. She ate flower pollen and drank the dew. The leaves on the trees protected her from the rain. The birds **sang** to her and . . .

. . . Thumbelina **sang** with them.

Summer passed quickly and before long the **cold** winter arrived. The flowers died and the leaves on the trees disappeared. The birds, who had cheered Thumbelina with their songs, flew away.

Now, Thumbelina was very sad and very **cold**.

Thumbelina wandered about in the freezing cold until she came to a field at the edge of the forest. In the middle of the field, she spied a mouse hole. She made her way to the doorway of the mouse hole and peered **inside** to find a whole room full of grain!

The lady mouse who lived there saw the poor freezing girl at her door and cried, "Poor child! Come **inside** my cozy, warm room and have dinner with me."

Thumbelina went **inside**.

The mouse told Thumbelina she could stay with her for the winter. In exchange, Thumbelina would help with the housework and sing songs, which the lady mouse loved.

One afternoon, the mouse told Thumbelina, "My neighbor will be visiting us today. He is a very rich mole. If he likes you, he might even marry you. Then you will be well taken care of for the rest of your life!" She went on to say that her neighbor was blind and he never went out into the sunlight. "But I **think** you could get used to that, Thumbelina."

Thumbelina did not **think** so.

Later that day, the neighbor **mole** dug his way over to the mouse's house and heaved himself up through her floorboards.

The lady mouse asked Thumbelina to sing for the **mole**. When she sang, he immediately fell in love with Thumbelina's exquisite voice. He told Thumbelina that he would like to **marry** her, but . . .

. . . she did not want to **marry** the **mole**.

The mole invited Thumbelina and the mouse to come and see his magnificent underground home. He led them down a long, dark tunnel, lighting the way with a glowing stick, which he held in his mouth. "Don't be afraid if you see a bird lying in the tunnel," he told them. "He must have fallen in and died here not long ago."

His words made Thumbelina feel very sad. She thought this bird might be one that had sung to her last summer.

Thumbelina became even more sad when they came to the spot where the bird lay. It was a swallow and his lovely wings were pressed lifelessly against his sides. He had surely died from the cold. The mole shook his head and said, "At least he won't be chattering away in the trees next summer. How awful to be a bird!"

Thumbelina fell to her knees beside the bird.

She gave the bird a big hug.

Thumbelina pushed aside the feathers on the bird's head and placed a kiss on his closed eyes. The bird's head was warm and Thumbelina wondered if the bird might still be alive. "Leave it," said the mole. "Let's go!"

Thumbelina did not want to go.

That night, Thumbelina could not sleep. She went back to the spot where the bird lay and wrapped him in a blanket, trying to warm him. "Please don't be dead," she said to the frozen bird. Then she placed her head against the swallow's chest and was startled to hear his heart beating! He was not dead after all!

Thumbelina was so happy!

The swallow told Thumbelina that he had hurt his wing and could not fly to the warm south this winter. Thumbelina made the bird a sling and the bird stayed in the tunnel until his wing was healed.

When spring came, the swallow asked Thumbelina if she would like to go north with him. But Thumbelina knew that it would make the lady mouse unhappy if she left, so she decided to stay.

"Goodbye, lovely child," said the swallow as he flew off toward the sun.

Thumbelina was very sad to see the bird go.

The lady mouse **told** Thumbelina that the time had come for her to marry the mole. Thumbelina told her she did not want to marry the mole, but the mouse would hear none of it. "Mr. Mole is an excellent catch. You should be happy that he has chosen to take care of you!" she said. "The wedding will be at the end of the summer. We must start preparations for it now."

Thumbelina did as she was **told**.

Thumbelina **began** to work, sewing the things she would need in her marriage. The mouse demanded that she work all summer long, making clothes and linens. At the end of the summer, the mole came for her.

Thumbelina knew he expected her to live with him beneath the earth, never again emerging to see the warm, beautiful sun.

She **began** to cry.

Thumbelina went up to say one last **goodbye** to the sun. With a heavy heart, she stepped from the doorway of lady mouse's home and raised her arms to the bright, summer sky. "**Goodbye**," she said.

"**Goodbye**, sun!"

"Tweet, tweet, tweet!" Thumbelina heard the sweet sound of a bird above her head. It was the swallow she had helped last winter.

The young girl told the bird of her sorrow and the bird said, "I am leaving today for the warm south. Come with me. Climb on my back and we will fly far, far away from here."

"Oh, yes!" said Thumbelina.

"I will go with you!"

She sat on the swallow's back, with her feet on his outstretched wings, and the bird flew up into the air. Together they flew above forests and over the sea and across large cities.

They flew very far.

The swallow flew on and on until at last they came to a **beautiful** palace. It was made of shiny marble and was surrounded by magnificent trees. Flowering vines twisted gracefully around its columns, and at the very top were many swallow's nests.

"This is my **home**," said the swallow. Thumbelina smiled.

It was a **beautiful home**.

"If you would like, you can live here in the flowers below my home," said the swallow. Then he set Thumbelina down on a large petal.

Thumbelina was so happy!

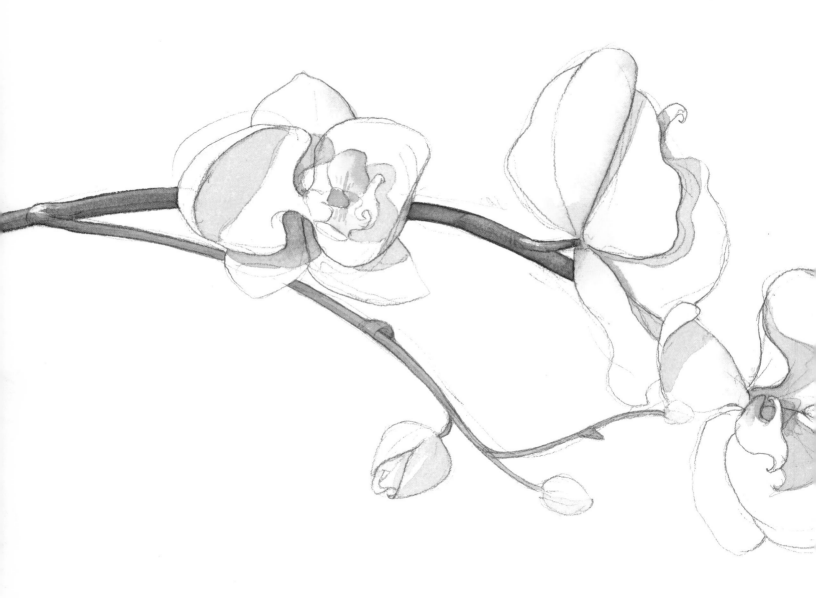

Then Thumbelina saw something in a flower nearby. It was a tiny man, no bigger than she was and very handsome! On his head was a golden crown and on his back were gorgeous crystal wings.

Thumbelina was a little frightened at first. But the tiny man was very kind and he told Thumbelina that she was the loveliest girl he had ever seen. He told her he was a **prince** of the flower kingdom and that he had been looking for someone just like her for many years. He said he hoped that Thumbelina would marry him someday and be a princess by his side.

Thumbelina thought this kind and handsome **prince** was certainly quite different than a slimy frog, a furry mole or a mean bug.

She liked the **prince** very much.

As the days passed, Thumbelina and the prince realized they loved each other very deeply and decided to get married. On the day of their wedding, Thumbelina and the prince were joined by the other tiny people who lived among the flowers. Each one brought a present for Thumbelina. The finest of these was a pair of wings, which **could** be attached to Thumbelina's back.

Now, she **could** fly!

The swallow, far above in his nest, sang his sweetest songs for them. It was a glorious day!

Soon it was time for the swallow to leave for the north once more. As a wedding gift to Thumbelina, he promised to visit Thumbelina's parents and to make his nest in their window. From there, he would sing to them all summer long, to let them know that their tiny Thumbelina would live happily ever after.

The End